GOING WEST

JEAN VAN LEEUWEN
Pictures by THOMAS B. ALLEN

Dial Books for Young Readers New York

Published by Dial Books for Young Readers
A Division of Penguin Books USA Inc.
375 Hudson Street | New York, New York 10014

Text copyright © 1992 by Jean Van Leeuwen
Illustrations copyright © 1992 by Thomas B. Allen
All rights reserved
Printed in Hong Kong
Design by Atha Tehon
First Edition

5 7 9 10 8 6

Library of Congress Cataloging in Publication Data
Van Leeuwen, Jean.
Going West | by Jean Van Leeuwen; pictures by Thomas B. Allen.
p. cm.
Summary: Follows a family's emigration by prairie schooner
from the East, across the plains to the West.
ISBN 0-8037-1027-5 (trade)—ISBN 0-8037-1028-3 (library)
[1. Frontier and pioneer life—Fiction. 2. Family life—Fiction.]
I. Allen, Thomas B. (Thomas Burt), 1928– ill. II. Title.
PZ7.V3273Go 1992 [Fic]—dc20 90-20694 CIP AC

The full-color artwork was prepared with charcoal, pastel,
and colored pencils. It was then scanner-separated and reproduced
in red, blue, yellow, and black halftones.

To the memory of all those brave families
who left their homes to find a new life, going west.
J. V. L.

For Melissa and Louis
T. B. A.

One day in early spring we packed everything we had into our wagon, tied our milk cow Sadie on behind, and set out to find a new home. Going West.

There were five of us: Papa and Mama;
me, Hannah, just turned seven; my little
brother Jake; and Rebecca, a fat baby with
yellow curls.

Mama cried. She was leaving her three
sisters and all our furniture and the piano she
loved to play. But Papa said we were going
to a place where anything you planted would
grow and a farm could stretch out as far
as the eye could see.

We left behind the town we knew, the woods,
the hills. We rode, bouncing and swaying in
the creaking wagon, day after day.

At night Mama cooked over a campfire
and we slept close together on the wagon floor,
with stars winking through the opening in
our canvas roof.

Here is what was in our wagon: blankets and pillows and quilts, Mama's favorite rocking chair, trunks full of clothes, barrels full of food, a cookstove, a box of tin dishes, all of Mama's cooking pots, all of Papa's tools, a Bible, a rifle, and a spinning wheel.

There was barely room for us.

Sometimes it rained. Our wagon got stuck in the mud and we all had to get out and push. Once it rained so hard that the wagon leaked. That night we slept in wet clothes in wet beds, without any supper. Rebecca cried, and Jake said he wanted to go home. Mama didn't say anything, but I think she felt the same.

We were all tired of the rocking wagon and the dust and the same sights day after day. Jake fell out and hurt his arm. Rebecca caught a cold. At night she coughed and coughed. Mama looked worried, but still we rode on.

Going West.

We came to a river, all muddy and wide.
"How will we get across?" I asked Papa.
"The horses will take us," he said.
First the water came up to the horses' knees.
And then their chests.

Suddenly Papa shouted, "Hold on tight!"
The horses were swimming. Water was pouring
into the wagon. Mama held me tight, until at last
I felt the horses' feet touch bottom again.
We had crossed the river.

On the other side of the river the land was flat, with no trees. There was not a bush and not a stone; nothing but green, waving grass and blue sky and a constant, whispering wind.
It seemed a lonely, empty place.
But Papa said, "This is the land we've been looking for."
As the sun was setting, we came upon a place where wildflowers bloomed in mounds of pink and lavender and blue, like soft pillows.
"Look," said Mama, smiling.
And Papa said, "Here is where we will build our house."

The next day we began. Papa took the
horses and rode away. When he came back,
he brought logs from the creek. For many days
he worked. Slowly, with Mama helping, he
built walls, a roof, a door.

Finally he took Mama's rocking chair and set it next to our new fireplace. It was only one room, with dirt for a floor, but at last we slept in a house again.

Mama planted a garden. Jake carried water from the creek to do the washing. I minded the baby and swept the dirt floor and helped Mama hang checked curtains on the window.

"There," she said. "We are ready for visitors."

But no visitors came. We were alone on the vast prairie.

Papa rode away again, many miles to town.
For three long days we watched and waited.
And then Papa came back. He brought flour
and bacon and six sheep that he traded for one
of the horses and a surprise: real white sugar.
Mama baked a cake and it reminded me
of home.

Summer came. A hot wind blew.
Papa went out hunting for rabbits, and
Jake and I picked blackberries next to
the creek.

Mama lay down in the grass with the
sheep.
"Oh my," she sighed when we found her.
"This is a lonesome land."

Day after day the sun beat down, baking our little house, shriveling up the plants in the garden. It was so hot that nothing moved, not even the wind.

"If only we had a tree for shade," said Mama.

One afternoon when Jake and I were at the creek, dark clouds suddenly covered the sun. Thunder rumbled and lightning flashed. We ran for home. But before we got there, hail came tumbling out of the sky, big and round and hard as marbles.

"Quick!" I shouted. "The buckets!" We put them over our heads and kept running.

Mama was waiting at the door. "Thank goodness you're safe," she said.

When the storm was over, Mama's garden was squashed flat. "The land is good," she said. "But the weather is hard."

"Never mind," said Papa. "In the spring we will plant again."

Mama was frying donuts and Jake and I were doing our lessons on the dirt floor, when visitors finally came: Indians! Jake hid under the bed. I crept behind the rocking chair, my knees trembling with fright. They looked so fierce.

But Mama smiled. She gave one of the Indians a donut. The Indian smiled. Mama kept on making donuts and the Indians kept on eating donuts until Papa came home. And then the Indians went away.

The wind turned cold. Mama stored up
potatoes and berries and nuts for the long
winter to come. Papa went hunting for deer.
He came back with Mr. Swenson. Mr.
Swenson stayed for supper and afterward
he played his flute while Mama sang, sitting
around the fire. And suddenly the prairie
wasn't empty anymore.

We had a neighbor.

"Do they have Christmas out here?" Jake asked. And I wondered too.

But Mama said, "Of course."

So we hung our stockings by the chimney. Rebecca got a cup and Jake a whistle and I found Nelly, a rag doll with yellow braids. Later we had wild turkey for dinner and Mama opened the jam she had been saving all year.

And everything was just like Christmas.

Now the icy wind seeped through cracks in our log walls. We put on all the clothes we had and huddled next to the fire. One morning it was so cold that Mama's fresh-baked bread was frozen solid. And then it began to snow.

It snowed for three days and three nights. Papa tied a rope from the house to the stable so he could feed the animals.

Jake and I did our lessons and Mama
helped me sew on my quilt and we all listened
to the wind howling outside.

At last everything grew still. Looking out,
we saw no woodpile, no stable, no sky,
nothing but snow drifting up to the roof of
our little house.

It was a long, cold winter. We had nothing to eat but potatoes and hard biscuits and nuts. Rebecca cried because she was hungry. And one day Mama counted the potatoes and said, "There are only six left."

But then slowly the snow began to melt. Each day the drifts under our window grew smaller. Papa took down his rifle and went hunting again. And that night the smell of rabbit stew made our house warm once more.

One morning when the grass was turning
new green, Papa said, "It's planting time."

He hitched our horse to the plow and broke
through the tough prairie grass to the dark,
rich soil beneath. For days he worked, plowing
long, straight rows. Then Mama dropped in
seeds and Jake and I covered them up. The
warm sun shone. The seeds sprouted. And all
around us, as far as my eyes could see,
was our farm.

It was Mama's birthday. Jake and I picked flowers for the table. Papa brought home a surprise: a little tree from the creek to plant by the front door.

"Next year if the corn does well," he said, "we will buy a piano."

And Mr. Swenson came for dinner with another surprise: his new wife.

"Welcome to our house," said Mama.

We ate Mama's food and listened to Mrs. Swenson tell about back East and sang, sitting around the fire. Outside, a soft wind was blowing in the new corn.

I looked around at Mama in her rocking chair and
Rebecca sleeping and Jake leaning on Papa's knee.
And our house felt like home.